AROUND THE WORLD

Edited By Megan Roberts

First published in Great Britain in 2018 by:

 Young**Writers**

Young Writers
Remus House
Coltsfoot Drive
Peterborough
PE2 9BF
Telephone: 01733 890066
Website: www.youngwriters.co.uk

FOREWORD

Young Writers was created in 1991 with the express purpose of promoting and encouraging creative writing. Each competition we create is tailored to the relevant age group, hopefully giving each pupil the inspiration and incentive to create their own piece of work, whether it's a poem or a short story. We truly believe that seeing their work in print gives pupils a sense of achievement and pride.

For Stranger Sagas, we challenged secondary school pupils to write a mini saga – a story in just 100 words. They were given the choice of eight story starters to give their imaginations a kick start:

- "Ouch!"... Instead of blood there were wires...
- "I need to stop," I whisper to myself...
- The mist clears and my name's on the moss-covered gravestone...
- We'd agreed on three meeting places, I'd just reached the last one...
- I remembered his last words: "This is the beginning of the end..."
- They say I'm a traitor...
- A scream echoes outside...
- "You have one chance, choose wisely..."

They could use any one of these to inspire their story, or alternatively they could choose to go it alone and create that all-important story starter themselves. With bizarre beginnings, mysterious middles and enigmatic endings, the resulting tales in this collection cover a range of genres and showcase the talent of the next generation. From fun to frightening to the weird and wonderful, these mini sagas are sure to keep you entertained and take you to strange new worlds.

CONTENTS

Institut Montana Zugerberg, Zugerberg

Nathalie Berndt Kristiansen (14)	48
Travis Matthew Seymour (13)	49

Kilchuimen Academy, Fort Augustus

Erin Surkitt (13)	50
Ruaraidh MacDonald (15)	51
Julina Cameron (13)	52
Katie Drummond (14)	53
Sam Kennard (13)	54
Louise Michelle Michie (15)	55
Willow-Mae Rowles (13)	56
Laura MacDonald (15)	57
Emma Rowe (13)	58
James McAllister (13)	59
Jack Andrews-Hall (13)	60

Mathematical Grammar School, Belgrade

Luka Jovičić (18)	61
Ilija Anastasijevic	62

Norwich School, Norwich

Alice Platten (12)	63
Spencer Harry Gray (11)	64
James Henry A Woodhead (11)	65
Anson Chan (12)	66
Tilly Hill (12)	67
Dilly Hockings (12)	68
Kaitlin Wolmarans (11)	69
Jonathan Ikazoboh (11)	70
Ralph Pye (12)	71
Sebastian Doe (12)	72
Tom Clark (11)	73
India Rose Bayes (12)	74
Benedict Pegge (11)	75
Daniel Conway (11)	76
Elliot Anthony Hawkings (12)	77
Matthew James Pethick Hudson (12)	78

Eliza Prior (12)	79

Pakefield High School, Pakefield

Will Jefferies (12)	80
Jess Scott (12)	81
Niamh Howard (12)	82
Ellie Collier (13)	83
Hannah Grace Wicks (11)	84
Maisy Rachael Eade (13)	85
Adam Mills (12)	86
Oliver Kane (13)	87
Molly Libby Crisp (13)	88
Finley William Dale (12)	89
Paige Kilduff (11)	90
Taylor Le Grice (12)	91
Sophia Allison (12)	92
Tia Brown (13)	93
Malachi Lawson (13)	94

Parkside Academy, Ipswich

Ryan Wayne Frederick Clarke (14)	95
Charlie Humphreys (15)	96
Jean Claudiu Vandam Pitigoi (16)	97
Catelyn Steward (16)	98
Tyler Woodley (16)	99
Toby Snowling (16)	100
Harry James Smith (14)	101
Elisei Hurmuz (15)	102

Portree High School, Portree

Dominik Heward (15)	103
Jessica Scott Moncrieff (14)	104

Ridgeway Independent School, Louis Trichardt

Ndivho Sorisa Mukoma (12)	105
Aazra Aboo (12)	106

Rolivhuwa Denicia Maphalaphathwa (12)	107
Zoe Mufaro Kamera (13)	108
Makhadzi Kutama (12)	109
Orifha Kutama (12)	110
Connor Christie (12)	111
Raniyah Bambawala (12)	112

Saint Dominic's International School, 2785-001 São Domingos De Rana

Maria Luiza Cardoso (17)	113

St Anne's School, Alderney

Poppy Taylor (15)	114
Connor Osborne (13)	115
Amelie Carpenter (12)	116
Yasmine Tate (15)	117
Erin Atkinson (13)	118
Star O'Connor (13)	119
Zack Eastwood (14)	120
Michaela Jane Cosheril (12)	121
Heather Syer (13)	122
Owen Carre (11)	123
Kamil Bruno Olbrycht (13)	124
Jess Coleman (12)	125
John Nellist (13)	126

Stour Valley Community School, Clare

Grace Frances Kidby (12)	127
Freya Grace Pitson (13)	128
Josephine Bursell (13)	129
Emil Bayazit (12)	130
Sophie McDowell (13)	131
Ryan Dunne (12)	132
Oliver Graham (16)	133
Ryleigh Bareham (12)	134
Eloise Holt (14)	135
Jamie Green (15)	136
Chloe Gridley (15)	137

Grace Robinson (12)	138
Jessica Sibley (12)	139
Madaline Amy Smith (15)	140
Vaughan Brinkman (15)	141
Tanya Smith (14)	142
Alfie Bojko (12)	143
Grace Brookes (12)	144
Callum Dalziel (11)	145
Zoë Bareham (15)	146
Maria Hanagan (12)	147
Shae Girvan (15)	148
Callum Devereux (12)	149
William Chapman (12)	150
Toby Cawston (14)	151
Sophie Paton (13)	152
Jon Ryan (14)	153
Jessica Eden-Shulver (13)	154
James Field-Rayner (15)	155
Hugo Hertz (13)	156
Aeryn Nicoll (15)	157
Piper Finch (15)	158
Amber Robins (14)	159
Liam Hircock (12)	160
Bradley Musk (14)	161
Ellie Allsup (14)	162
Calum Steven Hayward (12)	163
Sarah Warbis-Rodda (11)	164
Jez Perry (13)	165
George Clerkin (15)	166
Harry Neads (13)	167
Edward Chapman (11)	168
Katie Green (13)	169
Millie Wix (11)	170
Sid Holmes (13)	171
Kale Anthony Aaron Woodley (15)	172
Darcy L'Estrange (15)	173
Jayce Manning (15)	174
Thomas Chaplin (14)	175

Swans International School, Calle Lago De Los Cisnes

The International School Of Moscow, Krylatskoe

THE MINI SAGAS

The Stormflash Key

There's a noise coming from the basement. I don't like it.
What if it's a monster, after 3,000 years? Something's up.
Dad should've been back by now so I'm phoning him with
the payphone. That's weird. He's not answering.
"Hello, little girl," someone behind me says. "What are you
doing here? No, don't answer. This complicates things, but
it's a minor flaw. I'll take you with me!"
The payphone crackled. Rain poured down. The man
disappeared, and with him went the only thing preventing
the monsters from closing in. The thing no one's seen in
1,000 years: the Stormflash Key.

Abbie Howie (12)

Killing A Cure

I stood with the portrait in my hand, tears running down my cheek. I couldn't decide if they were from fear or anger.
"Be grateful," she said. In the dim kitchen, she seemed like a stranger.
"For what?" I spat.
"They were killed, Jack."
My breath caught in my throat. "Why?" I said, a mere whisper.
"We had no choice, they almost found the cure."
It was then that I noticed her luminescent green eyes and unnaturally arched back. She turned to face me and our eyes met. An eerie smile spread over her face. "Just a blessing in disguise."

Mila Casaleggio (16)

Unmasked

I just happened to be in the wrong place at the wrong time, or so I thought. I got off the plane, the terminal was empty. Where was everyone? Suddenly, I felt a sharp pain in my head, then it went dark.

"Where am I...?"

"You've seen too much," a voice whispered out from the dark. "They're coming."

A scream echoed outside. "What's happening?" I asked, desperate for an answer. In the dim light, the stranger removed her mask, revealing a tear-shaped birthmark underneath her right eye. What shocked me the most was that it was identical to mine.

Danya Casaleggio (14)

Thinking Time

They say I'm a traitor, but I'm just doing what's right. We were split into factions sixty-two days ago. They didn't like what I said so I'm sitting in a cold quadrilateral box with no windows. It smells of damp and human waste. They call it 'Thinking Time'. I was sentenced to ten days for rebelling against my faction leader. His name is August. Every day, my face is broadcast onto gargantuan television screens throughout the country, branding me a traitor. I hear the hatred through these flat walls. They are just sheep following orders. Isolated and alone, I contemplate.

Karys McIntyre (14)

Sea Of Flames

The inferno that swallowed the Earth struck an incomprehensible fear into my heart. As I stood at the viewpoint, sweat stippled down my body. A phantom heat seared my skin as if I was stuck on Earth.

"I'm safe," I whispered.

But the ghostly pain intensified. Screaming, I threw my arms around myself and shut my eyes. Opening them, I awoke on a scorching metal bed, surrounded by dozens of unconscious people. I looked up to find a screen live-streaming from the space station. Frantically, I whipped around to see a tidal wave of fire wrapping itself over the window.

Megan Soll (15)

The Strange Stare

The boy's face was always expressionless. I asked myself; was he staring at me out of curiosity, hatred or desire? He was in a world of his own. I often turned away. Every time I looked back he would meet my eyes with such an intense glare that I could feel my pulse thumping in my head. After two weeks, I marched over to his house only to find him sitting in a removal van. My teeth clenched.
"I'm glad you're leaving!" I shouted.
For the first time ever, he smiled at me and laughed as the van drove off.

Kate Gibbons (13)

I Have A Secret

This is me, a third-year at Marshalls High School, a perfectly normal girl, except I have a massive secret. I killed my mum and dad, well, my dad killed himself, but that was because he was heartbroken.

I was only ten, but my mum had a very painful stomach, so I went to get her some paracetamol at the shops, except it wasn't paracetamol I'd given her, it was a tablet a stranger gave me. Ecstacy. She was a very sensitive woman and she was unlucky enough to die because of it.

Promise not to tell anyone?

Rebecca Matheson (12)

Did You See It Too?

As I looked in the mirror, I was unsure what stared back at me; empty eyes, a fake smile... I don't know who I am any more, not after I saw it, it changed me.

I'd woken up one night to check on my baby sister; I'd heard her cry through the baby monitor but, as I got down there, she wasn't alone. An old woman, a ghost, was sitting beside her, using her as a puppet, pulling the strings. She looked at me and said, "I'll be back for her."

Since then, my sister has slept in my room.

Keris Nicole Clark (12)

The Horde

A scream echoed outside. I sat there with my heart beating out of my chest, my blood pumping with fear and adrenaline as I knew what was coming would wipe us out. I loaded a fresh magazine into my M4 and chambered a round. I automatically knew that thirty rounds of ammunition wasn't going to kill them all, but it meant that I could take some of them down with me. I stood up and disengaged my rifle's safety and watched the oncoming horde of creatures. I braced as I heard the terrifying roar that echoed in the mist.

Brandon Mckean (16)
Coatbridge High School, Coatbridge

Betrayal

"Ouch!" Instead of blood, there were wires.

"What?" I breathed, my brain struggling to comprehend the information my widened eyes were currently conveying. Wiring, cogs, pulsing lights, metal screws. All standard components found in a fully-functioning machine. But it wasn't a full-functioning machine I was looking at. This was my best friend's arm, and the dull shine of the unfamiliar mechanics peeking through her skin taunted me. I dropped the limb as if it had burnt me, eyes darting up to her deathly-pale face desperately.

"I'm sorry."

Tears slipped down her cheek as she shakily pulled out her gun...

Amelie Blanc (15)
College Jacques Monod, Les Pennes-Mirabeau

Pepperoni Pizza Or Mexican Food?

"You have one chance, choose wisely..."

"I think I'm gonna go with pepperoni pizza."

"I would've prefered the Mexican food..."

As Tom and Beatrice were discussing what they'll be eating tonight, they heard a crash in the corridor.

Tom decided to go take a look. At the second lighting bolt, a man emerged from the darkness. He started yelling and running at Tom. Tom immediately closed the door. Soon after, the third lightning bolt blew up the bulbs. While holding her in his arms, Tom heard a voice across the corridor, "It's all dark in here, where are you Tom?"

Marwan Saidi (13)

College Jacques Monod, Les Pennes-Mirabeau

Destiny

"You have one chance, choose wisely son," Delphia said.
"You betrayed father, do you think I have a choice, you soul eater?" I said.
"Soul eater? Do you know who you're talking to? Your mother, Death itself! Take back what you said right now and answer my question!" said Mother.
She was about to kill me, yet if I talked about Father, I was sure to face her wrath. I had to answer her.
"You wouldn't kill your son!"
"I could, but do I care?"
Her eyes turned black, she pointed her sharpened, ceremonial dagger towards me...

Coline Etesse (12)
College Jacques Monod, Les Pennes-Mirabeau

The Chosen One

"You have one chance, choose wisely."
These words chilled me to the bone. This terrible dilemma was an unbearable responsibility. I looked at these two entities, the mountainous weight of the world being carried on my shoulders. I could have lost consciousness, but I couldn't, not now.
At my right side, a golden sword was laying, illuminating my eyes and capable of defending the planet I was born on. On my left, a chip was there, improving my brain, I'd be able to dominate the invasion that was going on. My choice would determine the result of this intergalactic war...

Maelle Chiarello (14)
College Jacques Monod, Les Pennes-Mirabeau

Knock, Knock, Knock

A scream echoed outside the vast and desolate town, in which I'm the last one alive. Terrifed, I went to the door, cautiously bending down to look through the crack. Nothing.
Suddenly, there was another scream. I felt a damp, raw breath on my neck. Anxiously, I turned around. Still nothing to see, but something to hear. Another shriek echoed louder and closer. The tension filled my body. Slowly grabbing the handle, I opened the door and looked into the empty ruins. Nothing. Relieved, I went back to the room, sat on a chair, and waited.
Knock, knock, knock...

Felix Penna (14)
College Jacques Monod, Les Pennes-Mirabeau

The Seventh Garden

I remember Alex's last words, "This is the beginning of the end."

He had this weak, fake smile, just to reassure me before dying. Now, I'm alone, alone in the Seventh Garden. No one had ever gotten out alive of this paradise, that was actually a place of death. There was surely a way to escape, but what was it?

Alex was killed by the 'Night Terrors', the masterminds of the Seventh Garden who made sure that no one left this hell. Those creatures came every midnight to eviscerate new victims. I need to find a hiding place for tonight...

Lola Breham (13)
College Jacques Monod, Les Pennes-Mirabeau

The Day I Was Gone Forever

We'd agreed on three meeting places, I'd just reached the last one. I was alone. Everything was quiet except my heart beating. Something must have happened, I kept telling myself it wasn't my fault. It wasn't allowed to help 'enemies', but for me, they were only desperate human beings. I betrayed everyone to keep them safe. Maybe they were already caught? What could I do? Nothing. It was too late. My life was at risk. The only choice I had was to run away before someone discovered me. There was no point leaving a note, I knew they were gone.

Hanna Bouchama (14)
College Jacques Monod, Les Pennes-Mirabeau

The Impossible Choice

"You have one chance, choose wisely," Walter told me.
It was the biggest, most important dilemma.
"We have no more time Richard! Choose now!"
I was so stressed. For me, it was the end. I thought my parents would've killed me if I had made the wrong choice. At this moment, Walter, with his IQ of 197, determined which one was the fastest one by calculating all the possibilities that could happen.
Finally, we decided that it was the till on our left that was the fastest one. Actually, it was the other one that was faster...

Leo Goudal (13)
College Jacques Monod, Les Pennes-Mirabeau

The Choice

"You have one chance, choose wisely," said her best friend: a scientist who had created a portal to go to the past. Clara had two choices; the first, save her parents and lose her memory of the last three years, or let her parents die and keep her three years. Clara went to the past, but didn't save them because she wanted to keep what she had.
So, just before they died, she told them that she was happy and that she loved them. She swiftly entered the portal and came back. She told herself, "I've made the right choice..."

Ines Pascal-Galvis (11)
College Jacques Monod, Les Pennes-Mirabeau

Strangers And Secrets

We'd agreed on three meeting places. I'd just reached the third one...

I looked around the park, my eyes scanning for anyone who fitted the description she'd given me. When no one stood out, I sighed in relief, the sick feeling in my stomach dissolving.

I glanced down at the text she had sent me. How had she found out? Who was she threatening to tell? All my relatives had disappeared. I turned to leave, but found myself instead face-to-face with her. She smirked and everything went black, just like it had for the rest of my family.

Carys Blanc (13)
College Jacques Monod, Les Pennes-Mirabeau

Engraved Name

The mist clears and my name's on the moss-covered gravestone. I pass through this place every day, but this is the first time that I've seen this new tomb. I continue my way home, with this strange impression of being followed. Entering my house, I go to bed, immediately trying to fall asleep. The memory of this grave eats at me. I'm awake from the lack of fresh air in my lungs. I'm still lying, but my body couldn't move. It's all gloomy and the air is hot and thick. I realise that I'm in my tomb, buried underground...

Maëlle Enora Perrier (14)
College Jacques Monod, Les Pennes-Mirabeau

The Mystery Of The Tomb

I remember his last words, "This is the beginning of the end."
I'll explain for you...
I was an archeologist, I'd found a tomb in Egypt which had
never been opened before. I was excited. In the big room,
there was a golden sarcophagus and, coming out of it, there
was a hologram. It represented me! I was now terrified. The
3D picture murmured, "This is the beginning of the end of
your life..."
Then it disappeared without a noise. I was petrified.
My alarm rang. I woke up and tried to move, but I couldn't!

Penelope Duhamel (12)

College Jacques Monod, Les Pennes-Mirabeau

Who Am I?

A scream echoes outside, loud enough to wake me up. I go back to sleep anyway. Later, I hear knocks on the door. It's 2am, time to wake up! At the moment I open the door, I realise I'm wearing a red skirt and nothing else! In front of me was an upset lady. Straight away, she asks, "What were you doing last night? I heard a scream coming from your apartment."
Then I get a flashback; I see myself fainting on the floor and everything becomes pitch-black. Suddenly, a stunning question appears to me, "Who am I?"

Raphael Honnet (15)

College Jacques Monod, Les Pennes-Mirabeau

Black Hole

"I need to stop," I whispered to myself. I was flying in my spaceship, far away from my birth planet. But, so far, this beautiful blue planet was attracting me. I couldn't resist, I flew towards it. Suddenly, I was taken into a dark hole. Remembering my training, I pressed the big, red button and activated the light speed by using my fingerprint and a retina scan. When the pull stopped, I reduced the speed of my ship, but I'd used all the fuel to save myself from the black hole. I was lost forever, in outer space.

Raphaël Grissonnanche (12)
College Jacques Monod, Les Pennes-Mirabeau

The Afterlife

The mist cleared and my name was on the moss-covered gravestone. "That's impossible, I cannot be dead," I said to myself. But I was feeling like something was missing. However, I didn't know what it was. Nevertheless, I was so confused that I didn't realised I was flying!
"I am dead! How am I going to go shopping now?"
Afterwards, I tried to haunt people, but it didn't work. Then I understood how to go through walls. At first it was quite funny, but after a while, I thought it was silly.

Jade Louvradoux (13)

College Jacques Monod, Les Pennes-Mirabeau

Hunger Vs Intuition

"You have one chance, choose wisely," is what I said to myself.

Thursday morning was when this horrible deed happened. I woke up, put on my glasses and looked at my alarm clock; 3.36am it said. I wondered why I woke up and felt a growl in my stomach. I went down the stairs, opened my fridge, and pulled out a plate of cookies. I placed it on the counter, closed the fridge, then all of a sudden...

Boom!

My front door flew open. My first thought was to grab a knife and head to the door, but...

Harout Albarian (13)

College Jacques Monod, Les Pennes-Mirabeau

The Whole Truth

They say I'm a traitor, but they don't know the truth. I've been keeping this secret for too long, and you need to know. That night, I came back late and I found my brother hiding my sister's dead body in our garden. He explained that she had accidentally hit her head on the table in a fight they had. I needed to protect him, so I said it had been me. Now I regret it. I'm already dead, if you're reading this, but at least you know the truth, and that's the reason why I wrote these letters...

Laïa Pascal--Galvis (13)
College Jacques Monod, Les Pennes-Mirabeau

The Dreaded Choice

"You have one chance, choose wisely..." His voice was calm and serious. He talked slowly and he looked straight into my eyes. My life was dependant on this choice. I had the choice between the Dark Forest and the Floating Island.
While trying to figure out which one was the best option, I noticed that the man was still looking at me. He seemed to grow more and more annoyed. I was still hesitating when the man hit the counter with his fist and shouted, "Just make a choice! They are just cakes!"

Melina Haddad (13)
College Jacques Monod, Les Pennes-Mirabeau

There's Something Down There

There was a noise coming from the basement. I crept down the stairs. It was dark because only the light at the end worked. I started to walk around the room: there was no sign of life whatsoever. I opened the cupboard; empty. I looked in the drawers; empty. Everything had vanished! Suddenly, I saw something go past. I thought it was only a bat. I moved towards the light, then I saw that thing again. It was the shadow of something or someone and on the floor, I saw blood. From that day on, nobody saw me again...

Annabelle Le Bouffant (12)
College Jacques Monod, Les Pennes-Mirabeau

Poor Little Snake

A scream echoed outside. I ran out to see who was screaming and I saw a pretty, little girl. I found a dead snake next to her. Before I said anything, she explained why the snake was dead.

"Well, I was playing in the garden with my dog, when this horrible snake arrived. When my dog saw him, he ran away. I took a stick, too afraid to touch the snake. Unfortunately, he climbed up to bite me. I started to scream and I threw the stick away. When I realised the snake had hurt his head, he was dead!"

Clémentine Fabre (14)

College Jacques Monod, Les Pennes-Mirabeau

The Creepy Toilet Sound

Amenadiel kept breaking people's trust. One day, he was walking and he heard a swift swish coming from his toilet. He went to see what was in the toilet and found nothing. He left and heard that same sound again and again. Each time there was nothing.

Amenadiel went to bed and then woke up in the morning, and went to the toilet. He couldn't see anything scary or creepy. But then, in a flash, the grim reaper said, "You keep lying to people. If you keep lying, you will be flushed away."

Raphaël Gerard Max O'Connell-Lumbroso (12)

College Jacques Monod, Les Pennes-Mirabeau

The Forest Of Darkness

A scream echoes outside as we enter the dark forest. The four of us are entering the woods. Each of us are in dismay. We had lost track of time. Suddenly, emerging from behind a big tree, a shadowy figure appears. As it gets closer, weird pictures appear in our minds. Some of us fight it, their fists clenched and eyes shut, others drop dead on the ground. I try to resist for a while and let the creature invade my soul and lead me to the extent of the woods, at the very limit of its power. Welcome home...

Elie-June Marie Gallo (12)
College Jacques Monod, Les Pennes-Mirabeau

My One Regret

They say I'm a traitor because of what I've done. My parents won't talk to me. My friends look at me like I'm a serial killer. I decided to go on a quest to erase this horrible reputation. The next day, I packed my bag with a sandwich and water and headed out. I left a note for my parents, saying I left to right my wrongs. The streets were empty, dark, and silent. I headed for the path leading to the dark building. I did all of this because I ate the last pot of Nutella...

Mariam Pigache (12)
College Jacques Monod, Les Pennes-Mirabeau

The Mystery Killer

The mist cleared and my name was on the moss-covered gravestone. Was I from the future, or did someone want me dead? My name is Johnny, I'm thirty-seven years old and I was born in Los Angeles.
I went to eat at a restaurant, and they gave me a raw chicken when I arrived. They told me to cut it in half, so I cut it and found a letter in the chicken. Then I went to my house and someone was in it. He said, "You will not survive the day..."

Romeo Diego Varnier (12)

College Jacques Monod, Les Pennes-Mirabeau

My Last Breath

The mist cleared and my name was on the moss-covered gravestone. Underneath, a word I couldn't make out, and the date '2nd March 2018'.
I woke up. The memories of my dream overwhelmed me. After getting up, I realised something was off. Someone was watching me. I glanced around the room. Nothing. At that moment, out of nowhere, a sharp, dagger-like pain launched into my back. The deep, crimson colour dowsed the carpet around me. Suddenly, I realised what the phrase on the gravestone was: 'Murdered, 2nd March, 2018'. Childhood flashbacks filled my head. Then, I took my last breath.

Imogen Button (12)
Diss High School, Diss

Devil's Voice

The mist cleared and my name was on the moss-covered gravestone. I whispered, "What? It can't be..."
A deep, devilish voice whispered in my ear, "You don't remember, do you?"
"What do you mean? What's going on?" I was trembling with fear. No one replied. It was silent, nothing but the deathly whistles of the deceased. I saw a tall figure in the dark. "Who are you?" I shouted. He was dead silent and didn't move or flinch. I secretly pulled out my phone and I dialled 99...
"I wouldn't do that if I were you."

Luis Garratt (15)
Diss High School, Diss

Killers

They say I'm a traitor. I disagree. It wasn't my fault. I'm programmed to obey my master's wishes, not my own.
I was at the rustic, oak table in the middle of the opening hall when I caught a glimpse of Edward, sauntering through the heavy, dark, oak doors. The metal on my skin pricked as a hand slowly closed around my neck. I felt my body swiftly being lifted and thrust forward at my previous master. I saw him fall to the ground as the blood dripped from my blade, my life going with it.

Carla Oslavio (14)
Diss High School, Diss

The Last Words

I remembered his last words, "This is the beginning of the end." The last words he ever said to me. This was like a new chapter of our melancholic life without our favourite person. But eventually, we all go to that faraway place everyone dreads, but this is worse. He left at such a young age, with no proper goodbye from him. But you see, he taught me everything. He was my life and my idol. He had a real heart of gold. No one could ever change that. You see, he was my brother.

Rosie Reeve
Diss High School, Diss

Tales From The Front Line

"What am I doing here?" I wonder for a moment. "What's the purpose of me fighting in this war?"

I stand there for a while, deafened by the blasts from shells and blinded by the smoke and shrapnel, propelled in the air. "The enemy trenches are near!" cries the sergeant. "Charge!"

I stand up, pointing my bayonet at the enemy, fearlessly lunging myself towards them. The toxic clouds of chlorine gas sweep among us like foul ghosts. Our eyes start tearing up. In this vague reality, I ask myself, "Are we fighting to die, or to survive?"

Geo Kalfov (13)
First Private School Of Mathematics, Sofia

Last Chance

Two vein-like paths stretched before me. Gnarly trees surrounded them like talons, reaching out in the darkness. Both paths were identical, but I had to choose. Wings flapping like drumbeats echoed behind me, *thump, thump, thump,* mirroring my heart. Beads of sweat formed on my forehead. I chose. Left. Diving onto my bike, I raced like lightning away from the thing. Suddenly, a bellowing, explosion-like roar shook the branches. I turned around. Seconds later, I was lying on the cobbled pavement. My head pounded. I closed my eyes, not noticing the shadowy figure looming above me...

Emily Yardy (14)
Hobart High School, Loddon

The End Is Near...

I didn't understand what he meant. I asked him with desperation. *Beep.* He was gone. I fell down onto my knees, sobbing, hot tears poured down my face. That moment had been engraved into my brain. Everything always seemed to come back to his last words, "This is the beginning of the end." Suddenly, a mug fell off the side of the marble counter.

"Who's there?" I slowly crept over, ready to defend myself. I noticed a piece of crumpled paper. Cautiously, I opened the cocoon of paper. I was shocked to find, 'The end is near' scribbled in capitals.

Mia Barron (12)
Hobart High School, Loddon

Death Awaits

My heart stops. Am I underneath the ground? The only sound is my heart beating and the wind eerily rustling leaves. I may be paranoid, but I think someone is watching me. My eyes and ears dart around, noticing every movement and sound. Suddenly, someone pushes past me, it's getting dark, so I can't make out their face.
The mist has started to come back and the mystery person trips on the overgrown brambles snaking across the ground. They land face down. I walk over to them, holding a knife in my pocket. I then realise who it is...

Faye Hoggett-Thompson (14)
Hobart High School, Loddon

Humanity

Wires sprouted from the cut like a bouquet of electric flowers, bright sparks flying like a sword on a grindstone. I made a hurried attempt to conceal it but Ellie's eyes were sharp and her movements too quick. She gripped my arm with long fingernails and brought it to her face for closer inspection. I complained loudly, assuring her I was fine. Her piercing grey eyes looked at me as she dropped my arm and retreated to stand with the others. I was confronted with a trio of hurt faces that looked at me like I didn't belong.

Amelia Stephen (14)
Hobart High School, Loddon

Gravestone Tears

The mist cleared and my name was on the moss-covered gravestone. It silently screamed my name, as if it was begging for mercy. The mist strangled the stone as it slowly faded and I lost sight of it. I walked away with my lip trembling as if I'd never moved.

As the mist crawled across the grass towards me, my heart dropped as the moon awoke from its slumber. By now, the screaming souls were climbing up my shaking knees. I felt it trying to drown me in sorrow, raising only to the heart. Then I opened my eyes.

Madison Millage (12)
Hobart High School, Loddon

The Dying World

"I need to stop," I whispered to myself. Our world was dying, as were the memories of the people I'd ever loved. In this life, my thoughts were distorted as I stumbled, weaving in and out of the trees. Yet, nothing haunted me more than the shadow skulking behind. Sweat ran down my face, making my vision hazy. I didn't know where I was, and I didn't know where I was going. The only thing keeping me alive was the incessant voice in my head, trying to convince me that someone was still out there.

Joy Heather Marriott (13)
Hobart High School, Loddon

The Grave

My eyes lit up in shock. I looked up and saw the front of a shovel. *Bang!*
I woke up confined to a small space with an aching face in the dark, filled with terror. I screamed for help. There was no reply. I moved my hands around, trying to get an idea of where I was. Then I realised that I was in a coffin. I panicked even more, banging my hands on the coffin violently. No one came. I accepted my fate. Then there was movement against the lid. The coffin flew open...

Alfie Kevin Budds (14)
Hobart High School, Loddon

Crazy And Wild

"I need to stop," I whisper to myself. My head is shaking as the sharp, hell-turning implement lays in my mad driving hands, the blood of my enemies rolls off the paint of the katana and onto the cold, marble, calm floor, giving some sense of death and madness nearby. This is all crazy and wild, my heart begins to speed up as I realise what God cursed me with and the chaos I caused. Slowly walking back through the past machine, I spectate my wasted past...

Joshua Greest (12)
Hobart High School, Loddon

The Day That Went From Bad To Worse

My name was on a gravestone. Why was it on the gravestone? How did I die?

It all started two months ago when I got the job on board the Titanic. On my first day, I was so nervous that I was feeling sick. I was welcomed nicely by the captain.

A month later, I was on my way to the ship's captain when I felt a crash, followed by a scream. I was so scared! Then the captain came out and told us we had no choice but to jump.

Hannah Gavrila (12)
Hobart High School, Loddon

Home Sweet Home

My dad is a well-known, successful businessman who works at an insurance company. Everyone in town knows him. He's always helping somene and was awarded 'Most Considerate Civilian'. However, I know the secret that he keeps. It's a secret only my father and I know.
Every night, he comes home with another victim. He takes them downstairs to the basement, and that's where the screams echo from. It's there where he tortures them and makes it a living hell. My father is not a normal father, he is a murderer. If only other people knew, he could be stopped...

Nathalie Berndt Kristiansen (14)
Institut Montana Zugerberg, Zugerberg

Conversing With Death

"You got here quite quickly. That was a terrible way to end a story. But why should it be the ending? Why not make this the beginning?"

Death, the one ugly truth, stood before me. He asked me a question with an eerie grin, glancing at me with its hollow, empty eyes. His voice sounded like the wind howling in the darkest of woods. His body was slender, yet he had a firm and self-assured stance. He stepped closer, enough to unease me. He whispered quietly, "So, will it be the red pill, or the blue pill? Choose."

Travis Matthew Seymour (13)
Institut Montana Zugerberg, Zugerberg

3am

"I need to stop," I whispered to myself.
I slowly placed candles around the circle, tears flew down my face.
"I can't stop," I whispered as I placed my dead sacrifice on the floor inside my mark.
I proceeded to chant the words.
Angela!
I continued to sob.
Angela!
The pain won't leave.
Angela!
The pain stopped, my eyes closed, this was the end. No more shouting, no more suffering. It stopped. Everything stopped. Life stopped. I stopped. A hand extended. Was I dead? I took the hand as it dragged me into nothing. I was confused.
"Welcome, Angela."

Erin Surkitt (13)

Kilchuimen Academy, Fort Augustus

Who's Laughing Now?

Diary entry, day one: The end has finally come. Every country on Earth was firing nukes at each other. The booms have stopped now, but people were still banging on the door. They all laughed at me for building this bunker, but who's laughing now?

Diary entry, day seven: I started this diary so I wouldn't go crazy, but it's not working. There's something in the vents, something moving.

Diary entry, day fourteen: It's in the bunker! It's tall, and it can't be human. It's at my door, tapping the window, watching me.

Diary entry, day fifteen: "Who's laughing now?"

Ruaraidh MacDonald (15)

Kilchuimen Academy, Fort Augustus

It's Here

You can hear your heavy breathing echo through the forest. You try to continue, but you can't, exhaustion raided its way through your body. You slow down enough so you can lean against a tree. It's coming. Hollow scraping pierced through your brain. It's getting closer to you, you can feel it. The light from the moon illuminates its shadow, footprints start coming closer and closer. A shadow of long clouds grows across the trees. You don't know what to do, so you shriek so loudly, it knocks the leaves off the trees. It is in front of you...

Julina Cameron (13)
Kilchuimen Academy, Fort Augustus

The Nightmare Man

I was flat on my back in my bed, feeling traumatised. I'd woken up from a nightmare about the sound of someone throwing stones through my window. I had gone to the window, expecting to see my friends in my garden, but all I'd seen was a man with a black, hooded jumper. I gasped in fear. He'd heard me and spun his head round to my direction. He stared at me with eyes black as the night sky above, then smiled at me with a Pennywise smile.
"Luckily, it was just a dream."
My window then smashed.
"Hello Katie..."

Katie Drummond (14)
Kilchuimen Academy, Fort Augustus

Red Eyes

The sun disappeared over the crooked hill and we were engulfed in darkness. The house creaked. I tiptoed into the bedroom where the old monk perished. I saw a picture face down, and crept towards it, dodging the cobwebs. I picked it up and saw a monk; his nose bent, eyes red, jaw hanging. "I need to leave," I whispered to myself.

I dropped the picture and sprinted out. Slowly, a creature crawled out of the picture and stumbled towards me. I hid under a table, afraid. It crept into the room. It turned. Red eyes. Red blood. My blood...

Sam Kennard (13)

Kilchuimen Academy, Fort Augustus

A Grave Mistake

We walked through the graveyard on our way home. It was quicker. Ben looked at the graves, he was always more thoughtful that me.

"Aimee, look," he said, confused.

"What?" I turned around.

He knelt beside a moss-covered grave. I looked at it. My name was on it. I was scared about who was in it. Why my name?

As we continued home, Ben asked many questions, they flooded my mind. Why? I cleared my head of any other thoughts, all I wanted to know was who was buried with my name and with my photo. Who was it?

Louise Michelle Michie (15)
Kilchuimen Academy, Fort Augustus

You Have One Chance, Choose Wisely

This is the time; the beginning of the end. No turning back. I made this happen, it's my problem.

One day, a bad thing hapened, because of this, my life changed completely. I was visited by a dark force that found a way to put evil in me. This showed through my right eye changing it pure black. The same thing happened again, but instead of evil, it was light magic and then my left eye became pure white. Unfortunately, my friend got jealous and things would never be the same. I had to pick, the light or the dark?

Willow-Mae Rowles (13)
Kilchuimen Academy, Fort Augustus

A Painful Scream

A chilling scream rings through my ears. I bolt up, looking around for the source of the noise. I'm standing on cold, wet tar. I shakily make my way through the thick smog. Getting closer, I hear my name in a painful screech. It startles me. As I look in all directions, I notice that there is a lot of chewed-up metal lying around. I see a number plate, but its not just anybody's, it's mine. I start running, getting closer to the noise. I see my friend in distress, looking at my blood-steeped body on the road.

Laura MacDonald (15)
Kilchuimen Academy, Fort Augustus

Psychic

I'm a psychic. The worst thing to see is someone's death. When someone sees you, they sometimes ask for their death. I lied to a man about his life; I told him that he would die old. I wrote to his wife, telling her I saw him die in a car crash four months later. He did.
I got in the car with my wife and children, who were arguing. I tried to seperate them. I foresaw them both crushed by another car. I told my wife to stop. I tried to get the children out. The seatbelts were stuck.

Emma Rowe (13)
Kilchuimen Academy, Fort Augustus

My 18th Birthday

I was looking online for a car because my dad said I could have a car. After a while, I came across a reasonably priced Ford Fiesta. I messaged the person and asked if I could go over and check the car. The person said, "No problem."
I arrived at his house on my bike. It looked like no one was home, all the lights were off. I knocked on the door. No one answeered so I looked through the window and a black figure stood there. I ran to my bike, but the black figure was stood there.

James McAllister (13)
Kilchuimen Academy, Fort Augustus

It's There But It's Not

Here I am, creeping out at the bottom of a crumbled castle. As the ground shakes, some sort of beast awakes. I run. Nothing is here, but there is. It's right behind me, but I see nothing. I wondered if it was an illusion. A scream echoes outside. I run back to the castle, the scream getting louder. I stumbled and gash my leg. I crawl to the door and swing it open. It's there in front of me. I blink in surprise...

Jack Andrews-Hall (13)
Kilchuimen Academy, Fort Augustus

The Final Warning

I remembered his last words: "This is the beginning of the end..." This morning, he didn't wake up. I thought, *no*, I was certain he was delusional. All those stories about tiny artificial creatures killing from inside sounded so surreal. Now I know my every breath can be the last one. The thought of having all my tissues ripped apart by beings I can't even see is indeed much more terrifying than any visible monster. I know tomorrow won't be much different than yesterday, only quieter. Yet, all I can do is hope someone out there will find the cure.

Luka Jovičić (18)
Mathematical Grammar School, Belgrade

Delta-V

In space, objects in motion stay in motion. I am closing the distance to the malfunctioning ObSat III at a rate of 50 meters per second. I need to turn around and decelerate to avoid smashing my faceplate against the aluminium panel. I align my arm thruster and depress the switch. No effect. In about 7.5 seconds, I will impact the satellite at great speed. I attempt to fire lateral thrusters and dodge, but my suit's propellant valve stays shut. *I really, really need to stop!* is the only thought I can muster before I hit the satellite's antenna array.

Ilija Anastasijevic
Mathematical Grammar School, Belgrade

I Hate Horror Okay?

They say I'm a traitor but I only did what seemed right in my heart. It was my fifteenth birthday, I was entering the family tradition - watching horror movies. I walked into the darkness and shuffled to the shelf. I couldn't hold myself back, 'Love Actually' was next to 'IT'. I thought they wouldn't notice, they did. I've never been into horror, I'm more of a comedy or romance kind of girl. I sat down. They asked, "What's wrong darling?"
"I hate horror, okay?" I shouted. They stared at me blankly. I stood up, feeling triumphant. I was victorious.

Alice Platten (12)
Norwich School, Norwich

McDonald's Or Subway?

"You have one chance, choose wisely," that's what my friend said.

McDonald's or Subway, you decide. At Subway, there's a three-pound deal; a drink, six-inch meatball Mariana, cookies. But at McDonald's, a Big Mac and medium fries are two pounds fifty. But they both have big queues. Subway has slightly worse food, but the cookies are amazing! I also really like Big Macs. What should I choose? This is a life or death situation...

I chose the wonderful, delicious McDonald's. Yum. I love this, wait a second. I'm thirsty, I need a drink! I chose wrong!

Spencer Harry Gray (11)
Norwich School, Norwich

Diary Of A Dead Man

"I need to stop," I whispered to myself. This was the fifteenth murder I'd committed this week, but I couldn't stop, not if I knew what was good for myself. I'd already seen how ruthless they were, they didn't bluff. I couldn't fight them, there were three of them and one of me. The trouble? I'm good at murder. I can walk into a room of a hundred people, kill one and walk out before anyone knows what's happening. A thought just came to my mind, I can murder but my captors can't. I'll sneak into their hideout, blades drawn...

James Henry A Woodhead (11)
Norwich School, Norwich

The Decision

"You have one chance, choose wisely." His heart pounded as he stared at his friends, who had knives at their throats. The battered clock ticked in the lamp-lit room, which put even more pressure on him. One of his friends wept in despair, trying to get free. It was too late, the thief drew his knife along his friend's neck, blood spilling from his veins. The murdered man dropped to his knees and fell onto the stone-cold floor. "Choose!" Sweat dribbled down his bruised cheeks, followed by a tear that was made of pure sorrow. He said the words...

Anson Chan (12)
Norwich School, Norwich

Doctor Day!

"I need to stop," I whispered to myself. Sweat trickled down my back. The heat of the sun, it was all too much. I turned my head, a cricket ball, hit by my partner, came right at my head. I tried to dodge it but I was too late.

Next thing I knew, I was in hospital with a crowd of doctors surrounding me. They were taking me into another room, the sign on the door said: *Way to cemetery*. I felt someone shaking my shoulder.

I opened my eyes to see Archie, my brother, shouting, "Wake up! Today's Doctor Day!"

Tilly Hill (12)
Norwich School, Norwich

Decisions

"You have one chance, choose wisely. Your next move could be the difference between moving on to round two or death," said the voice in my earpiece as I hid behind a boulder, bullets raining down on us. "Do you throw the grenade and hope or sit there waiting for their ammo to run out? Make your choice."
My head was spinning, I couldn't think clearly. I could remember that they'd raised the bullet supplies just days before. They weren't going to run out any time soon. I got up, pulled the pin and then threw the bomb. I missed.

Dilly Hockings (12)
Norwich School, Norwich

The Decision Would Change My Life Forever!

"You have one choice, choose wisely," a voice echoed behind me.

I stood there, my heart beating, hands shaking and sweat running down my face. Another breeze came from behind me as people kept on making decisions. It was a busy time in this heavenly place. There were so many choices. I couldn't decide, how could people do this? The decision would change my life forever. If one of them vanished, what would I do? I grabbed two items and went to the till. "Which one should I have? Crunchie or Twirl?" I said to my mum.

Kaitlin Wolmarans (11)
Norwich School, Norwich

The Decision

"You have one chance, choose wisely." I should have thought about it before it had become a distant memory. I was obstinate, holding onto senseless ties, thinking that everything would be fine after that day. I was wrong...
All I do is wait, wait for someone or something to help my broken self. I am just being selfish. It was my fault after all, I broke myself. I made it happen. I'm just hopeless, an unwanted drag. All I do is think that the world revolves around me, but it's because of that thought that I lost her...

Jonathan Ikazoboh (11)
Norwich School, Norwich

KFH (Kentucky Fried Humans)

"You have one choice, choose wisely." That's what the KFC manager told me, but as I eyed up the menu, I had no idea what was good and what was bad. But when I told him I would just have a McDonald's, he said, "No you're not!" and locked the building. The server drew a knife. I screamed, but it was no use. Then I realised the sickening truth, KFC wasn't a chicken industry, it was a human industry. That's why there were no customers. They ran out of chicken years ago. I felt the blood on my neck...

Ralph Pye (12)

Norwich School, Norwich

The Mission In DR Congo

"You have one chance, choose wisely," the guard snarled. The undercover spy used his thirty years of experience to knock him down with one blow with his foot. Then he saw it. It was practically in reach, but there was something blocking it. A black mamba. He wasn't sure what to do. He could crush it, but it was not likely to die. He looked for any other entrance into the crypt but it was just a solid, concrete block. While he was thinking, he wasn't thinking about the creature in front of him. Then, the snake struck.

Sebastian Doe (12)
Norwich School, Norwich

Murder Across The Road

I remembered his last words, "This is the beginning of the end." I brushed away the damp, vibrant leaves to reveal the sandy, Aztec temple glittering in the new-found sunlight. Then I saw them, the orange and...

I woke up in a heavy sweat and contemplating the events of my dream. Swiping the curtains away, I saw the house on the other side. Still tired and sleepy, I didn't notice anything unusual at first. Then I realised there was a crowd of people outside the house. I slipped on my clothes and ran outside...

Tom Clark (11)
Norwich School, Norwich

Cottesmore Leap

"I need to stop," I whispered to myself, "I've worked so hard for this, I can't quit now. Come on Halla, we can do this girl." Her Palomino ears flickered back and forth, listening to me, trusting me. It was approaching fast now, the toughest fence on the Burghley Horse Trails course, Cottesmore Leap, the fence with a big drop in the middle. She was tiring and I knew it. I was risking both of our lives. Three strides, two, one, we were in midair! Halla's legs crumbled like jelly beneath her...

India Rose Bayes (12)
Norwich School, Norwich

STRANGER SAGAS - AROUND THE WORLD

Decisions... Decisions...

"You have one chance, choose wisely," is what I heard her say. How could I choose it so easily? It seemed an impossible task to me. My future depended on my decision today. All I could think about was how this choice would lead to my future happiness or dread. Simple words, but such a task for my mind to get to grips with. Should I go with the obvious choice or should I try something new? The pressure was building, all eyes were upon me. How could I make the choice between Smarties or a KitKat? I didn't know...

Benedict Pegge (11)
Norwich School, Norwich

Not My Problem

They say I'm a traitor. Well, that's their opinion. As some people say, a man's got to do what a man's got to do. Selling secrets, not a big deal, not my problem. It's not *my* problem. They were the ones who left the plans lying around. If you had seen the place where I'd been living, you would have so much sympathy. It's worse than the sewers. When the day came to sell the secrets, I entered the North Korean Embassy in America. I heard a voice behind me, "Goodbye traitor."

Daniel Conway (11)
Norwich School, Norwich

Bad Dream

A scream echoes outside and I wake up, covered in sweat. A distant bell rings. I am hit by a wave of pain, my body rigid. Suddenly, nothing. Then I open my eyes and I'm in my kitchen. But not exactly. There is blood scattered on the floor, not only that, my relatives and loved ones are also there, littering the floor. Then darkness again.

Now I'm in my street, but the sky and ground are red with flames. Hot sweat covers my body and my insides can't take the heat. I feel dreadful. I wake up...

Elliot Anthony Hawkings (12)

Norwich School, Norwich

A Message For Our World

I remembered his last words, "This is the beginning of the end." I now wish I'd believed my father, because he was right. Even before the last county in England fell to dictatorship, the world was a horrific place. My innocent wife disappeared one day, I learned she'd been executed by our invaders. Our children and I were being hunted, we'd fled to the sanctuary of the forest in fear for our lives. The worst part was that we were no longer living, but waiting for the end...

Matthew James Pethick Hudson (12)

Norwich School, Norwich

Outcast In Charge

They say I'm a traitor. They sent me away. I have my new people. What will they say?

I was drowsy by midnight but I had to tell the chief why I had joined his clan. My air bubble came to me and I spoke. "I used to be an Earth-being in London. It was the year 3000 and I was the woman in charge. I made a vote for us to rejoin the European Union, but my people said I was a halfwit. They flew me here, thinking I would die."

Chief said, "Begin the hostile takeover!"

Eliza Prior (12)
Norwich School, Norwich

A Strange Occurrence

My gran had been drop-kicked out of the tree. Then I remembered I was playing PlayerUnknown's Battlegrounds. I realised that it was the worst game ever made. They said I'm a traitor so I switched my PlayStation off and turned my Xbox on, Fortnite.
I played for hours on end. I finally got a kill. However, instead of blood, there were wires. What had happened? Then, I remembered I had colourblind mode on. I messed about with the controls and turned the sensitivity up to full. I changed to the Brazilian servers. I had gotten my first win!

Will Jefferies (12)
Pakefield High School, Pakefield

The Screams

A scream echoed outside, causing my knees to buckle. I waited, hoping I wouldn't be the next victim. Another scream pierced the still night air. I decided to run to free myself from this prison. This prison of screams. Ma wouldn't support me. Ma died. She was the first victim. I was alone on my journey. Alone in the wilderness, escaping the monsters that ate my ma.

The forest grew unfriendly, threatening. I tried to run faster, but I couldn't. I heard the howls, I heard the screams of my friends. I knew they were coming for me...

Jess Scott (12)

Pakefield High School, Pakefield

The Graveyard

The mist, thick, eerie, and never-ending. I was walking through the graveyard because I had nothing better to do. I was all alone. My friends didn't want to come. They didn't like the graveyard. It had something different about it. I didn't like to think about it. I kept on walking. Everything seemed normal. Suddenly, the mist cleared. Right in front of me was a gravestone with my name on it. Was it a relative with the same name as me? I just kept staring at it. *I'm sure I'm not a ghost. I can't be, can I?*

Niamh Howard (12)
Pakefield High School, Pakefield

Into The Mist

The mist cleared and my name was on the moss-covered gravestone. Instant panic ran throughout my body. How did I get here? Where was I? Why were my friends not here with me?

It was a muggy night and the graveyard was silent. I hadn't been here before and I wasn't planning on staying too long either. I wandered all around, trying to figure out how I'd gotten myself into this situation. I was trembling by this point, scared of what my next move would be. I looked up at the jet-black sky when suddenly, it all made sense.

Ellie Collier (13)
Pakefield High School, Pakefield

My Gravestone Story

The mist cleared and my name was on the moss-covered gravestone.
"This can't be happening!" I fainted.
I had ten missed calls from my mum and twenty text messages. I looked at them: 'Where are you? It's teatime'. I walked home and, when I got home, it was silent. All of a sudden, I heard a crash. I walked into the living room. I couldn't see anything at first. A door swung open, nobody came out. I saw a shadow. I screamed and ran upstairs and tried to wake up Mum and Dad. Nothing...

Hannah Grace Wicks (11)
Pakefield High School, Pakefield

Deathly Daggers

I was in the graveyard, my skin covered in goosebumps. My name was engraved on the mossy stone. Suddenly, a fuzzy feeling took over my body. A cold hand pressed on my shoulder. I turned my head slowly and saw a fearsome creature with blood dripping from its teeth, sharp as the blade of a dagger. It crawled closer towards me as I slowly backed away, cutting my hand on the grave as I walked. I felt the damp moss on my back and the beast skulked towards me. Closer and closer. *Crunch!* Its teeth sunk into my flesh...

Maisy Rachael Eade (13)
Pakefield High School, Pakefield

Zombie Dinosaurs Vs Space Vampires

There once was a cat who got hit by a car. The cat turned into a spaceman and the woman got out of her car and the spaceman sucked her blood.

On the other side of the universe, a dog was hit by a digger, but it was still alive. It became a dinosaur. Then he was shot in the face, becoming a zombie! He craved cat brains and that made the space vampire angry.

They had a massive fight, but the universe became unstable. Everything disappeared and the planet they were fighting on was left. Everyone had died.

Adam Mills (12)

Pakefield High School, Pakefield

The Graveyard Terrors

The mist clears and my name's on the moss-covered gravestone. My heart stops. Fear runs down my spine as fast as light. I can hear the deceased under their misty grave. The fear kicks into me, speaking to me, saying, "Run Robert, run!" I instantly start to pick up speed. The fear of being taken to the other side is petrifying. Suddenly, I see hands rising up from the boggy ground. My speed picks up. I can see the entrance. Hoping I will get there in time. Hoping I'm not too late!

Oliver Kane (13)
Pakefield High School, Pakefield

The End Begins...

I walked on into the distance, trying to find a way out of here, but it was impossible. I'd been told thousands of times that no one had ever gotten out, but I wanted to be the first one. I wasn't going to die alone, I would feel afraid, lonely, disturbed. My family would be worried about me and where I'd disappeared to. I hoped nothing would happen to them, like it did to me. I was banging on the door when suddenly... *creak!* A tall, manly-shaped figure came towards me...

Molly Libby Crisp (13)
Pakefield High School, Pakefield

When Gaming Goes Wong

We'd agreed on three meeting places, I'd just reached the last one. I was on my Xbox and PC but I was pretty sure this was not my house. I was scared and worried. I knew there was something wrong. I heard something that sounded like my favourite game, Fortnite. The winning sound. I looked around the corner and I saw someone in black with a knife. I thought he saw me. I needed to get away. I saw a hut and hid in it. I was frightened. I heard footsteps. He was there. He was outside...

Finley William Dale (12)
Pakefield High School, Pakefield

One More Chance

"You have one more chance, choose wisely." I remembered when I was in the graveyard. I was walking along the damp path as the wind blew into my face. Then I saw it on the stone: *You have one more chance, choose wisely.* I remembered that I had to either cut my hand and then kiss the blood, or I had to go to the haunted house that no one had visited in 3000 years. If I didn't do either of them, then I would haunt everyone. But which one should I choose?

Paige Kilduff (11)
Pakefield High School, Pakefield

Alien

A scream echoed outside. I went to check it out. It was some sort of being. It looked horrifying. It had a massive spine, long tail, really tall, sounded alien. Then, the alien left. I checked to see who screamed and it was my neighbour. He was chopped up and eaten. I heard the alien come back again and I hid. The alien started to sniff the ground for my scent so it could track me down. The alien got really close, then I heard a noise. There was another alien...

Taylor Le Grice (12)
Pakefield High School, Pakefield

The Day Death Visited Me

The mist cleared and my name was on the moss-covered gravestone. I realised that my name was written in blood. A whisper came from the forest to tell me, "Your fate lies in a tomb." I started to run but wherever I ran, the forest was there to greet me. Something was following because the voices were getting louder. The voices from the grave. I knew that wherever I ran to, death would be there to greet me. Today was the day I was going to die.

Sophia Allison (12)
Pakefield High School, Pakefield

The Disappearing

We'd agreed on three meeting places. I'd just reached the last one, no one was there. What was I meant to do? How would I get home? I thought that if I went back the way I came, I wouldn't get lost. I went back and got lost. There were two glowing circles in the distance, were they eyes or lights? I went to investigate, but when I got closer, they disappeared. I saw a pile of leaves and as I stood on top to see, they had gone...

Tia Brown (13)
Pakefield High School, Pakefield

A Knight In The Field

One dark night, on the Friday 13th of April, Mandem the baker went out to feed the scarecrow. Bread was getting too much for the scarecrow, he had a seizure and souls from Hell came to him. They told him to kill the baker or be forced to eat bread forever and ever. The scarecrow was scared. He got the meat knife and hid it under his arm. Eventually, the baker came out and the scarecrow killed him, but then, the scarecrow died.

Malachi Lawson (13)
Pakefield High School, Pakefield

The Forest

You have one chance, choose wisely, the sign in the pitch-black forest read. "Let's just go home. It's just too weird," Ryan said bluntly.

"No, don't be stupid. Let's just take the path on the right. It'll be fun!" Patrick laughed.

"Look, we've got no signal anyway. Let's just go back the way we came," pleaded Ryan.

"See you later then, I'm going," said Patrick, slowly walking down the dark, zigzagged path.

A couple of seconds later, Ryan followed. He couldn't let his friend down, could he? But that would be the last time anyone saw Ryan and Patrick.

Ryan Wayne Frederick Clarke (14)
Parkside Academy, Ipswich

The Basement

A scream echoed outside. Ana was creeping through the woods, hoping she wouldn't be found. Unexpectedly, she tripped over a rope and was sent hanging high. "Help!" Ana loudly cried. Kerry followed the scream and turned back around to see Ana dangling upside down from the tree, blood dripping from her mouth, nose and ears. Kerry discovered a trapdoor hidden beneath the leaves. She went in.

Walking down the tunnel, she revealed a massive room full of traps and children hanging from the ceiling. Suddenly, the trapdoor slammed shut, trapping Kerry inside. A little girl's scream echoed inside...

Charlie Humphreys (15)

Parkside Academy, Ipswich

Hunger!

"I need to stop," I whispered to myself, my jaws biting the remaining bits of hair and bones. Do vampires really need human flesh to survive? I was living proof that it was not true. I was a teenager in high school, an ordinary, regular kid. You name it, I had it. No one ever imagined an ancient vampire was in their school. Waiting. Watching. Wanting. I'd wrestled and brawled with my demons for decades and I'd had enough. I had to confront them and defy them once and for all. I just didn't want to consume humans...

Jean Claudiu Vandam Pitigoi (16)
Parkside Academy, Ipswich

Men In Black

You have one chance, choose wisely, the sign said. How did I get here? What happened to me? Where was I?
Twenty-four hours earlier, I'd been out with my friends in the woods, walking our adorable dogs. Suddenly, we came across some men all dressed in black. We were so petrified. We ran the other way, but, after a while, we heard heavy footsteps close behind. I turned around and the noise disappeared. The trees were swirling, I was so terrified. We ran again, the footsteps started again and I heard a loud bang...

Catelyn Steward (16)
Parkside Academy, Ipswich

The Dream

"You have one chance, choose wisely..." The words echoed around in my head. What do they mean? I'd had the same reoccurring dream for days, weeks, months. I'd lost count. But the dream always ended the same way, hearing those fateful words, making me anxious, insecure and confused. Every day was the same: get up, go to work, finish work, go home, repeat. Sounds boring, right? Wrong. I was a gangster and there was nothing wrong with my life. That was my routine. Well, it was until the dreams started...

Tyler Woodley (16)
Parkside Academy, Ipswich

The Butcher

"I need to stop," I whispered to myself as I dragged victim number 167 upstairs in the shop. I used to be smart, clever even. I remembered at primary school I felt like I had a brain. But then it all went wrong. Here I was, looking into the dead, lifeless eyes of a young school child. However, it wasn't just any young child. This was the child of the man who made my life a misery. His life was about to get more shoddy than it ever was. A butcher's revenge was delicious.

Toby Snowling (16)
Parkside Academy, Ipswich

The Scream

A scream echoed outside. I was scared. I was on a school trip in Sussex, lying in bed. My bed was underneath the window, which always freaked me out. I've always been worried that someone would break in and attack me. As soon as I was about to drift off, a bone-chilling scream echoed out across the fields. I nervously looked out the window and saw nothing but lights in the pool. Everyone went outside and saw a tall, shadowy figure dragging a large body-shaped bag into the forest...

Harry James Smith (14)
Parkside Academy, Ipswich

The Crash

I remember his last words after the accident, "This is the beginning of the end." I had jumped out of the car, he was stuck because the door was blocked. I was in shock, twisted metal ripped the car apart. It was unrecognisable. I didn't know what to do. I had been speeding and I had been distracted by my phone. We'd hit the Central Reservation. The car was crushed, I pulled him out of the car. I called an ambulance, it was his last breath...

Elisei Hurmuz (15)
Parkside Academy, Ipswich

The Cave By The Sea

I crawled into the cave. The sounds of running water and falling pebbles echoed around me. The wind blew its way in, howling like a wolf. I struggled on. Suddenly, I heard a dog bark. A deep, threatening growl. On impulse, I barked back. It replied. As we barked back and forth, I carried on deeper into the narrowing cave. Uneasily, I looked at the disappearing opening behind me.

Without warning, the cave came to an abrupt end. I fumbled around. There was no dog, only the rushing tide hurling in. To my horror, I realised that I was trapped.

Dominik Heward (15)
Portree High School, Portree

Beginning Of The End

The beginning of the end has begun. My world is not what it used to be. I feel empty, my voice bounces off the walls in my head. I'm screaming, but no one can hear because I'm completely alone, like I'm trapped between the numbness and the hell I've built inside.

I wake up every morning, hearing the same voice over and over again, screaming how worthless I am. I can't decide what's better: to keep feeling so unbelievably alone, or to give up. Then I see the light hit me... Everything goes black.

Jessica Scott Moncrieff (14)

Portree High School, Portree

Bad Dreams

Instead of blood, there were wires. Instead of partying, there was screaming. Fear and despair clouded my eyes.
"Shh."
What was that poking into my sweater, ignoring my pulse? I tried to be oblivious, but the further I walked, the more hands I felt, the more shouts and screams I heard. Monsters, beasts, zombies, snakes, spiders, small spaces, ever single fear I had popped around me.
I walked faster. I breathed heavily. I tried to look for somewhere I could hide or seek help. Nothing. Nothing at all, except for the gracious voice of my mother awakening me.

Ndivho Sorisa Mukoma (12)
Ridgeway Independent School, Louis Trichardt

The Mist

Stacey saw the mist creeping up. She stood there, silently still. Suddenly, she heard a voice saying, "Breathe in the mist."

She was too scared to look back. Then Stacey heard the petrifying voice again, but this time, it was louder and more clear. Stacey felt a cold hand on her shoulder. She then felt an ice-cold breath on the side of her cheek, followed by the words, "Breathe in the mist and feel the transformation." Her feet felt bolted to the ground. She was paralysed with fear.

What is going to happen to me? she thought to herself.

Aazra Aboo (12)
Ridgeway Independent School, Louis Trichardt

The Cemetery

I ran because I found it very creepy. As I stopped, I saw something interesting. It was a bat. I walked towards it and it screeched as it flew into my face. My life flashed before my eyes.

As I blinked and my eyes opened clearly, I saw an exit sign and ran for it. A surprisingly pretty thing stopped me, saying, "You've got one chance, choose wisely: go and get your mom, or go home."

"I'll leave, thank you."

"I said, go and fetch your mom!" it shouted.

"No."

It slapped me hard and I woke up in shock.

Rolivhuwa Denicia Maphalaphathwa (12)

Ridgeway Independent School, Louis Trichardt

Choices

They say I'm a traitor. Why? Well, let me start from the beginning. It all started on the last day of school. My friend, Theresa, invited me over to her house. That made my friend, Maddie, jealous. During the holidays, Maddie wouldn't even come to my house or even look at me when we saw each other in shops. One day, she finally talked to me. She asked me to be friends with her, but to stop being friends with Theresa.

"You have a choice, choose wisely," she said.

I chose carefully and chose Theresa. Maddie wasn't a good friend.

Zoe Mufaro Kamera (13)
Ridgeway Independent School, Louis Trichardt

Incomplete

More words began to form on the gravestone and it said *incomplete*. I began to run, running was all I could think of. I tripped over a rock which transformed into 'The Beast'. It was so terrifying, at that moment, I knew I'd die. The mist became thicker and thicker when the words on the gravestone changed. *Incomplete homework*. I stood and saw the rock-like homework books, and I saw my teacher standing there with a frown on her face. I was in detention, but I promised to do my homework and I definitely will not be here again.

Makhadzi Kutama (12)
Ridgeway Independent School, Louis Trichardt

What Came First

There I was, pinned to the ground, with my mother's life in my hands, screaming, "It's going to be okay!"
I knew it wasn't because if anything, I knew I wasn't dumb. Our kidnapper asked me a life or death question which had bad consequences: if I got it wrong, my mom died, if I got it right, we got to live. The question was hard, like, really hard. It was confusing and it was really stressing me. A nice holiday gone bad. The question he had been asking me was, "What came first, the chicken or the egg?"

Orifha Kutama (12)
Ridgeway Independent School, Louis Trichardt

Killer Mist

It all began at the graveyard. It was my two friends and I, we were pranksters, trying to mess up the graveyard. We started by spray-painting the headstones. We thought that nothing bad would happen, but we were wrong. Mist came out of nowhere, we were starting to hear whispers, then the ground started to crumble, hands were coming out of the ground, trying to grab our legs. We ran like the wind. One of my friends tripped and got pulled into the mist. We ran home. Finally, I got home and reached for the door handle.

Connor Christie (12)
Ridgeway Independent School, Louis Trichardt

Strangest Thoughts I Feel!

One day, I was walking in the school hall. I thought I wasn't alone, every step I took, the more I felt like someone was there. I felt as if I was tangled in a spider's web and every time I said something, the spider would creep out.
I heard the screech of chalks as if someone was angry and taking it out on the blackboard. I actually thought it was a ghost. I thought that over several times, but as soon as I saw papers flying around the classroom, I knew I had to run!

Raniyah Bambawala (12)
Ridgeway Independent School, Louis Trichardt

Death Quest

I kept telling myself, "This is only one of life's games, I'll get out of this nightmare as soon as possible..."
Suddenly, out of the howling blizzard they came... Three hooded figures with dripping candles in their hands. As they flipped back their hoods, I immediately recognised them: they were my family! A heart-aching thought came to my mind: what would become of them now? Was this the price they should pay? I promised them I would come home alive. Now, this served as a warning to survive all of my missions and fight against my fate...

Maria Luiza Cardoso (17)
Saint Dominic's International School, 2785-001 São Domingos De Rana

The Answer

Died June 7th, 2018...
My mind ran in all directions, uncontrolled. A muffled, ominous voice emerged from the darkness.
"Find out how you died and prevent it from happening!"
Terrified, I didn't know what to do, apart from stand there like a stiff goat, a sleepwalking creature without focus, without hope.
Slowly, I walked from the gargantuan, metallic, rusted gates, before being suddenly faced with an old-fashioned, mountain-topped house. Paralysed with fear, I traversed the blustery, bumpy drive. I turned the doorknob and I was faced with the mirrored image of myself. Was this the answer?

Poppy Taylor (15)
St Anne's School, Alderney

Deadly Conflict

Zoom! My metallic ship zipped out of this perculiar solar system. *Bang!* A star destroyer joined me in this now awkward situation. What was I to do? My puny ship against their gargantuan monstrosity they called a ship! Suddenly, the walls began to shake as their tractor beam latched onto my vessel.

Panicking, I reached out, jabbing vigorously at the hyperdrive button, still shaking and infused with anger at the dishonourable Empire. A noise, that started at a drone, built rapidly. The tractor beam, pulsing visceral energy, fought my hyperdrive in deadly conflict. Who would win?

Connor Osborne (13)
St Anne's School, Alderney

The Outcast

I prefer to refer to myself an outcast, someone who undeniably doesn't quite harmonise with their community. Why do they see me like this? It's all because I'm different. You can tell that they all despise me. They've tried their very hardest to conceal it, yet I still take notice. The whispers behind my back, the crossing of the street when they see me heading their way. Even the babies, newborn babies hate me with a passion, they bawl their eyes out at the sight of me. This is why I'm abandoning this town, ending the nightmare...

Amelie Carpenter (12)
St Anne's School, Alderney

The Night Of The Zombie Clown

The mist cleared and his name was on the moss-covered gravestone. When suddenly, something touched him on the shoulder, he turned around and saw the zombie clown. Bob started screaming. The zombie clown was holding a red balloon saying, "La la la, you're going to die."
Bob ran through the graveyard, getting chased by this horrible, dead creature. Then Bob tripped over a tree stump. The clown pushed Bob into a coffin, put him underground, and started to bury him in the mud. The clown then carved Bob's name onto the gravestone...

Yasmine Tate (15)
St Anne's School, Alderney

I Need To Stop!

"I need to stop!" I say in a quiet voice. I need to stop these uncontrollable persuasions to 'break out' of this 'slammer'. however, I don't know how. In iron chains, I'm a hostage. I want my life back. I must figure out a way to escape this torturous house, but I can't find it. Escape this beast-like creature before it's too late. I am confined, locked away. Does anyone remember me beyond these walls? All I know is that there is little time left and I wish I could see you again. I mustn't get caught...

Erin Atkinson (13)
St Anne's School, Alderney

Nightmare

I turn around and standing there is my worst nightmare. I try to run, but my body won't move. As his thunderous steps get closer, sweat starts dripping down my forehead. His dark shadow, now towering over me, makes me shudder. Fear runs through my body as I feel his hot, steamy breath touch my smooth skin. I attempt to run again, but he grabs my arm and pulls me right back into him. I look up into his bloodshot eyes. He assertively stares right back into mine. He whispers to me, "Any last words?"
He raises the knife.

Star O'Connor (13)
St Anne's School, Alderney

The Fog

Never before had I seen this: wires as thin as tendons. As I eyed up the neck, removed from the decapitated head, I felt the dark sky become darker, the cold air become colder. I surveyed my surroundings; the moon had become minute, foreshadowing our fate. A gale was brewing. Our end was coming.

As I looked more intently, fog entered the scene, black in colour, cold to the touch. however, this was no natural fog. Strangely, it suddenly became easier to see ahead now; to see the tank approaching. We turned to run, but it was too late...

Zack Eastwood (14)
St Anne's School, Alderney

The Creature

They say I'm a traitor...

They are the traitors, not me. Everyone gripped onto spears or bows, chanting as they bounded towards me. I couldn't tell you exactly what I created, however I just knew that one day, they would find me and we would discover new worlds together.

They had extensive, rose-red wings, their vision as marvellous as that of a fearsome falcon with eyes as green as emeralds and claws sharper than sharpened knives. They said I was psychotic for spending my life creating this, but they would see, they'd see the mistake they made...

Michaela Jane Cosheril (12)
St Anne's School, Alderney

Déjà Dead

I know it is wrong, but I can't, I can't help myself. I feel a rush, one that I have never felt before, but somehow I have. Déjà vu. I live for the motion. I lie for the thrill of it. Like a snake, it coils around my aching bones, keeping me half dead, yet somehow living. I am but an itch, a pain in your world but you still have to keep digging; find the truth. Sometimes it hurts like one thousand daggers have been viciously thrust into your chest. But not to me, your weakness makes me stronger.

Heather Syer (13)
St Anne's School, Alderney

Wires

Dangling down from my arm, they fell about me. Wires, everywhere. I was scared. I didn't know what I was. Was I now a robot? A machine? Who or what had done this to me? Who wouldn't be confused? Muddled? In crisis? You see, there was no pain; my arm up to my elbow had been cut off, sawed off.

I didn't know what to do anymore, however the next morning, on waking, my arm was back to normal. Determined, I would not let this rest. I set myself a mission: to find out what was happening to my body.

Owen Carre (11)
St Anne's School, Alderney

I Tried To Escape

I tred to run when they came. The things slaughtered everyone who came in their path, even children and women. I ran straight to the safety exit when they invaded my district. Everyone there was crying all around me. I went through the fight to a big truck, barely any room for me to fit in. We went across the whole country to Maine.
Well, we attempted to get there. The aliens stopped us. I just barely got out from the mangled truck. I ran to the woods, going as fast as I can. That is all I remember...

Kamil Bruno Olbrycht (13)
St Anne's School, Alderney

Deal With The Devil

They say I'm a traitor...

I say I'm a survivor. They don't understand that the sacrifice had to be made, and they never will. No matter how often I explain that what I did was good, they are still convinced that I am evil. Why can't they just see it from my point of view? I wish they would just give me a chance to explain myself instead of forcing me to go on the run. Can't they see that I had to make a deal with the devil? For once, can't they just understand? I'm not close to what they see me as.

Jess Coleman (12)
St Anne's School, Alderney

Instead Of Blood

The wires were black, blacker than an unlit night. The wires had begun to reside in my veins, growing bigger every second. They stopped suddenly and began to shrink again, contracting closer to my chest, which stabbed ever closer to my arteries, until the wire began to slowly spiral inwards. Wires persisted, pinning my arms and legs to the floor, straight through me, to reach my heart. Hitting the organ, it quickly detracted, stealing my heart.

John Nellist (13)
St Anne's School, Alderney

The Creature And Isabella

The creature explained, "Take the poison and you will forget your lover or you can live with the pain, stinging you like little needles stabbing your heart."

"I'm taking it," said the confident Isabella. "What do you want from me?"

"A strand of your hair," the creature cackled.

"Fine. What for? A new potion of yours?"

"You're correct. Love, the strongest magic in the world-"

"You're incorrect, creature. There is a stronger magic than love. Hate!" Isabella grabbed a dagger and stabbed him in the heart, wailing. He laughed.

"Did you really think you could defeat me?"

Grace Frances Kidby (12)
Stour Valley Community School, Clare

The Voices

"Shut them out, don't listen. They don't know you. They know your fears. Just don't listen." I was diagnosed with schizophrenia years ago. They said it wouldn't be too bad. They lied. The voices know my darkest secrets, my deepest fears, my broken promises and my evil lies. "I'm strong," I remind myself. "I won't let them break me." Then, I hear slurred voices getting louder and louder until they drown out every other noise. "Go away!" I scream. My voice echoes through the empty house. "You don't know me! I won't let you break me! I won't let you!"

Freya Grace Pitson (13)
Stour Valley Community School, Clare

Care - Not Control

Words whispered into my ear by my mother after my first 'proper' heartbreak. Believe me, I chose the wrong one. He entangled me in his web of lies and disguised isolation. "But he loves me!" *No.* "You don't understand!" *It was me who didn't understand.* "It's not your business!" *Silly girl.* Everyone knew but me. Like there was a big joke, but they forgot to tell me the punchline. When they tried telling me, I ignored them. It was my fault. I was blinded by his gifts. Mistook, 'where are you' texts as caring, not controlling. Wrong choices break you.

Josephine Bursell (13)
Stour Valley Community School, Clare

Destruction

The scream of a girl. The scream of pure terror... The world's destruction all started when a viral video of a petrified young boy was uploaded online. He was saying how 'they' were after him. 'They' were hideous. Drool dripped like long jewels. Teeth stained red, 'they' were horrid. The girl ran. Running away from the terror of the monsters. The adult monsters. Zombies even. Pus covered their pale, blotchy skin. Boils and scabs scarred the blistering remains of what used to be human beings. 'They' only wanted human meat, but in this world, who didn't?

Emil Bayazit (12)
Stour Valley Community School, Clare

The Day My Grandad Died

I stopped, tears running down my face. I remembered about the secret, the secret no one was meant to know. I got up and ran as fast as my legs would take me.

Finally, I reached home.

"What's wrong?" my mum said.

"They know, they all know," I replied.

"Know what?"

"About my grandad's death," I said sadly. I fell into despair, all I could think about was what was going to happen next? What would my friends think? What would my teacher think? My grandad was right, this was the beginning of the end of my dramatic life.

Sophie McDowell (13)

Stour Valley Community School, Clare

The Terrible Dream

"Ouch!" Instead of blood, there were wires. I stood still, thinking, *what am I?* "Argh!" I fell. More wires fell out. Coming back home, I shouted, "Why did you not tell me?" I walked into the lounge, seeing my mum and dad on the floor. Dead. *Flash!* I opened my eyes, finding myself lying in my bed. I looked at my body. "Am I human?" I said. I ran downstairs into the lounge. My parents weren't there. I wondered, "Where are they?" I went into the kitchen, seeing my mum.
"Pancakes!"

Ryan Dunne (12)
Stour Valley Community School, Clare

Guilty Or Not Guilty? To The Jury

Am I though? It's for you to decide. Let's see the evidence.
It was a winter's morning in Oslo, Norway. I was looking for
a mysterious ex-soldier called Markus Svergaard. He was
wanted by Intelligence Services for stealing and selling
Norwegian military secrets to America as revenge. I had to
find him.

By the end of the day, I was the one in a police cell. The
memory stick had been planted on me by Svergaard. He
hadn't been caught, so I was a traitor to Norway. It wasn't
my fault!

Jury members, it's up to you. Guilty or not?

Oliver Graham (16)
Stour Valley Community School, Clare

The Misty Graveyard

I had agreed to go and put some flowers on my uncle's grave. As I was walking through the graveyard, I was reading the names on the gravestones. It became foggy. As the mist cleared, a moss-covered gravestone appeared. It had my name on it. I started to hear footsteps approaching me. I ran. I didn't stop running.

As I approached where my uncle's grave should have been, all the names on the graves became mine. I ran home and into my room, thoughts rushing through my head. The main one was, *is it real or not?* I'd never know...

Ryleigh Bareham (12)
Stour Valley Community School, Clare

Invisibility

They seriously aren't my friends. I sit all alone, feeling isolated, wondering what I've really done. Am I invisible? Can you hear me? Am I dreaming? I question myself on a daily basis. However, when they actually speak to me, I act fine, I'm really not. They don't care do they? If I wasn't here, no one would actually realise, would they? In my old school, I got along with so many people and I always felt involved. Now I feel invisible, like I don't mean anything to anyone. "I need to stop," I whisper to myself...

Eloise Holt (14)
Stour Valley Community School, Clare

I'm No Traitor

They say I'm a traitor, I'm just trying to survive. You need to be your own man to stay one step ahead. Forget about friendship, forget about love, forget about family. If you start thinking for even a second, you will be caught, which you really don't want to happen. Prison is not nice, trust me, I've been there. It's like a constant war, you're always having to fight for your life, and when you go there, you won't get out. Please use the advice I've given you, there's no going back now. Be careful and good luck...

Jamie Green (15)
Stour Valley Community School, Clare

Was I Dreaming?

I thought I heard something, obviously not. I was in my picturesque cottage. It was usually peaceful outside, only the birds to keep me company. I heard another scream, this time I ventured out into the garden. I heard whispers of, "Molly, Molly, come closer." I stood still and pivoted on the spot. I felt firm fingers wrap around my shoulder, the smell was penetrating my nose. I screamed thunderously. I was yanked backwards. As I hit the floor, a hand clasped my mouth. I tried to scream, but there was nothing I could do now...

Chloe Gridley (15)
Stour Valley Community School, Clare

Hunted

I was panting heavily, my long tongue lolling like a dried up worm. I knew if I didn't stop soon, I would collapse. I took a large swig of water. Suddenly, pounding footsteps echoed painfully to my sensitive ears. It was them! They'd found me! Quickly but unsteadily, I rose to my feet and began to run. It was too late! A large hand grabbed hold of my hood and hoisted me into the air, leaving my bushy, orange tail scraping the cobbles desperately. I turned to face my captor. I was staring into the sneering glare of The Huntsman.

Grace Robinson (12)
Stour Valley Community School, Clare

The End Has Come

Now I knew what he had meant. *They* had come and they'd destroyed everything. I had watched in pure terror as they devoured my family, demolished my home. I just ran. I didn't know where to but eventually, I ended up in a dirty ditch, still trembling with fear. However, I knew that they'd soon find me. But I didn't know what I'd do when they came. At that moment, I heard a noise which stopped my heart. The robots had come for me! Slowly, I stood up, seizing the gun in my hand firmly as I prepared to fight.

Jessica Sibley (12)
Stour Valley Community School, Clare

Olympic Dream

My legs burn as they pound against the ground. Mist appears in my eyes. My heart thumps against my chest. Why did I do this? Stop and quit. Then I'd be a laughing stock, a failure! The daring Kenyan emerges by my side, the crowd shrieks. He sneers at me, humoured by my inner battles. Digging deep, a sudden bolt of lightning rips through my aching body, I rush forwards. I silence the cheers and concentrate on my pace. *One, two, one, two.* The voices in my head vanish, one hundred metres stand between me and a gold medal.

Madaline Amy Smith (15)
Stour Valley Community School, Clare

Contagious Ideals

They say I'm a traitor, but I don't feel like one. But then, I assume we never do. People, everywhere, should know what happens down here. That's what Dr McIntosh said to me, right before those cold men in their cold suits took him who knows where. I asked of course, but they said nothing. So now I wait to be taken as well. Inevitability is a word that continues to cross my mind. I hear footsteps in the corridor outside, a murmur of voices. I close my eyes as they take me, despite the action being one of pointlessness.

Vaughan Brinkman (15)
Stour Valley Community School, Clare

Living Life Alone

You say I'm a traitor, but really it's a case of I don't care. I don't believe in friendships, I don't even bother with love or family because after all, you'll die alone. All that's ever happened to me is being left for someone better! So why should I bother? They'll just stab you in the back!
Me? A traitor? Never. I'm just living life alone. Voices after voices, it's all that ever happens in my head. So, take this from me. I'm no traitor, I'm just confused. Really confused.

Tanya Smith (14)
Stour Valley Community School, Clare

The Abandoned

I can't go on. As I reached the entrance of the zoo, all my friends ran in front of me shouting, "Run!" They started climbing up the fence that said: *Danger!* in capital letters. Silverback gorillas were coming after us. There were sparks coming off the metal, wired fence. I started running towards the fence and climbing on it. One of my friends started shaking as he got to the top. He lost his grip and fell. I grabbed his arm tightly. I didn't let go, but his arm started to slip from my slippery grip.

Alfie Bojko (12)

Stour Valley Community School, Clare

Stabbed

They say I'm a betrayer of humankind. They say I'm black-hearted.
As I roamed around the gloom-filled, unwelcoming forest, the words echoed around in my lifeless mind repeatedly. Suddenly, I heard a head-splitting, deafening, howl-like shriek edging closer. Then I noticed it. A bruised, blue-coloured, battered head with the veins pouring with thick, oozing blood where the head had been detached from the body. The stabbed eye still had one teardrop left to cry. I wished this was a dream, but it was definitely real.

Grace Brookes (12)
Stour Valley Community School, Clare

The Last Defender

They say I'm a traitor, I laugh at this. They have no idea, nobody does. Nobody knows I was the last defender. Nobody knows how we fell. All except me. I haven't been accepted, not in my entire life. So I'm fine with being thought of as a traitor, a murderer. That's what they had to think. That's what ran through my head as I aimed. My finger rested on the trigger. My scope pointed to his head. I learned a long time ago, death was a blessing. So I pulled the trigger. Now he's a dead man, like me...

Callum Dalziel (11)

Stour Valley Community School, Clare

Long-Lost Sister

We'd agreed on three meeting places. I'd just reached the last one. After ten years, I was finally going to meet the sister I'd never had. I could see a small figure in the distance, which I assumed was her. I picked up my pace. I couldn't believe that I was about to finally meet her. My excitement was too much. My feet started to stumble around as I was walking. Suddenly, a strong hand pulled me back. I jumped, but I didn't stop. Nothing was going to stop me from seeing my sister this time. Nothing.

Zoë Bareham (15)

Stour Valley Community School, Clare

Running From Death

I smiled smugly, I knew deep down I was the one responsible for her death, but the murder was a mystery to anyone else. I could sense the terrible feeling of anger creeping up behind me, stealing my confidence. I stepped outside into the rustling rain to run from my fears. The piercing sound of the chiming church bells came quickly, before a grubby hand with peeling skin emerged from the wet soil, pulling me under by my ankles. The hand was owned by the angry girl I had just stolen the life from. She wanted her revenge.

Maria Hanagan (12)
Stour Valley Community School, Clare

My Grandad's Last Words

I remembered his last words, "This is the beginning of the end." My grandad said those words just before he died in hospital. I visited his grave and I remembered lots of things, like when my mum died and my dad left. I'd moved in with my nan and grandad.
Two months later, he got cancer, that was it. He was gone forever. What did he mean by 'the beginning of the end'? The end of what? His life? The beginning of what? His death? It was amazing how life could be over in what felt like seconds.

Shae Girvan (15)
Stour Valley Community School, Clare

"I Need To Stop," I Whispered To Myself

I couldn't stop it, but I needed to, fast. I just couldn't help myself, I kept playing on my games. Mum was shouting from upstairs, "Stop it! It will blow up!" I had kept playing for so long that the console was getting hotter and hotter. It was soon going to explode, but I couldn't stop playing. I was addicted. I was just having so much fun. *Bang!*
I was rushed to the hospital and didn't wake up ever again. I wished I had listened. Mum was right. I was such an idiotic person.

Callum Devereux (12)
Stour Valley Community School, Clare

The DD (Death Demon)

I was confused and oblivious to what was happening. "Jack! George!" I bellowed at the top of my voice. Then suddenly, a high-pitched whistle left me curled up on the floor like a puppy, the clouds growled at me and the gravestone was a wolf! I could just make out the rustle of a bush, I turned over, searching for my phone, but something chucked it at me. Then it emerged, it had a bear coat on its back, horns and a torn-up, blue face. It prowled, then grabbed me and chucked me into the grave. It laughed.

William Chapman (12)
Stour Valley Community School, Clare

Choose Wisely

The leader of the robbery chose me as his second, it was tough. I could only choose one getaway driver, who would have one chance. I was convinced I'd chosen wisely.
We rushed off to the jewellery store and waited outside. Was it alarmed? Did it have security guards? We didn't know, we were going in blind, had to be in and out in one minute. We charged into the store, held everyone at gunpoint, took as much as we could, then charged out and headed to the car. We had one chance. Had I chosen wisely?

Toby Cawston (14)
Stour Valley Community School, Clare

Hurt

The snow lay thick and peaceful, almost like a blanket. The air was dense and dry, like sandpaper. Then there was my heart. Nothing. For so long, I tried to understand how life could be so bittersweet, to understand how something so amazing could change or even be destroyed in a matter of seconds. I felt a lump in my throat, then the next thing I knew, there were tears oozing down my rosy cheeks. I collapsed to the floor. "I need to stop," I whispered to myself. He was gone and was never coming back.

Sophie Paton (13)
Stour Valley Community School, Clare

Elite Thief

I'm only a traitor because I broke the rules that were destroying the world. Maybe I should tell you the backstory as to why everyone thinks I'm a traitor.

In 2047, there were many mutants. A law stated that you couldn't take supplies just for one person so I broke into a lab, stole a cure and injected it into my friend to make him good again.

Now, as always, we are running away from civilisation. I have shot thirty elite soldiers with a plasma gun I've stolen. This is my life now...

Jon Ryan (14)
Stour Valley Community School, Clare

Murder In The Woods

I stood over the body of an innocent person. "I hate this, I'm sorry, it's not my fault!" Blood dripped off the knife and the tips of my fingers. A cold shiver went down my spine as I stabbed the corpse one last time. I loosened my grip on the knife and fell to my knees, bursting into tears. "Why did you make me do this? He was innocent!" A figure stepped out of the shadows.
"You know what he did and if you didn't do it, your family would've joined that man!"

Jessica Eden-Shulver (13)
Stour Valley Community School, Clare

The Scream

Everyone should've been down the deserted streets, but weren't. Where were they? A loud noise came from the school. It was the scream again, suddenly it all stopped. Another scream, this one much louder and more scared than the first. I heard what sounded like a gunshot. Thoughts rushed through my mind of what had happened but I knew the only way to find out for certain was to go into the school. I walked in to see a clown with a gun! I ran, running until I fell. I lost all feeling. It was all over.

James Field-Rayner (15)
Stour Valley Community School, Clare

Last Breath

As I lay on my deathbed in tears, weeping, I hoped the angels from above would just take me now. My mum, my dad, my sister, my grandparents, everyone was gone. Only I survived. All of my 'friends' betrayed me, saying it was all my fault, asking why I did it.

From feeling the pain and depression inside me, I knew even the doctors around me couldn't save my family, so what belief was there that they could save me too? This was my time, I would not be on this world. This was my last breath...

Hugo Hertz (13)

Stour Valley Community School, Clare

Run

A scream echoes outside, which I take as my cue to drop out the tree house. I start running the second my feet hit the floor, pelting through the forest, trying to get as far as I can while it's still distracted. I reach an abandoned shack encased in a thick, electric fence. I scout each side of it until I find a hole which I edge through, careful not to brush against the sparkling edges. Vomit churns at the back of my throat as I bolt into the shack. I never should've come into the woods at night.

Aeryn Nicoll (15)
Stour Valley Community School, Clare

Revenge

I spoke through the speaker, knowing exactly who was on the other side. Their decision would ruin their lives. They'd already ruined mine. I doubt they would remember. They wouldn't remember me. Why would they? They didn't even know me back then, I was just an innocent child and they took away everything I ever wanted. I would do exactly to them that they did to me. "Make up your mind," my chilling voice said through the speaker. Little did they know, I would kill them all anyway.

Piper Finch (15)
Stour Valley Community School, Clare

The Mystery Offence

I suddenly felt myself shoot up from my warm bed, like a bullet shooting through the air. My forehead was soaked in a sticky, damp substance. A light was piercing through the crack of my door. I realised the damp substance was blood dripping down from a hanging body above my head. I heard myself wail.

Startled, I woke up, confined and confused, in an unknown space with a dampish cloth on my forehead. I had woken up in a world where I didn't know anything or anyone. Who was I? Where was I?

Amber Robins (14)
Stour Valley Community School, Clare

The Little Girl

Seeing a little girl crying in the grass, I drove down to see her. She was in ripped clothing, blood dripped from her eyes. I got out of the car and she leapt out at me. I got back in and she scratched at the window. Then, someone limped onto the roof. The door at the back opened, then someone got in, a featureless face, long with no emotion. I got pulled back and I got a scratch across my neck.

Then, I woke up, sweat across my brow, panting from the scare. I felt the scratch on my neck...

Liam Hircock (12)
Stour Valley Community School, Clare

The Mist

It sounded close so I looked out of my window and there was mist as far as I could see. I could only see to the front of my garden. I lived opposite a graveyard so I was worried something bad could have happened. I put my shoes on and walked over to the noise. I heard another scream so I walked quickly back to my house.

I was walking for ten minutes, I was lost, I felt claustrophobic from the thick fog surrounding me. I started to feel dizzy, then I passed out and never woke up again...

Bradley Musk (14)

Stour Valley Community School, Clare

A Scream Echoes Outside

I rushed outside but there was no one there. I looked around, but still no sight. It was strange because it sounded like it was outside my house. I fell asleep, another scream echoed. I shot up and looked out the window. There was a figure outside my house. I ran downstairs, opened the door, but still, no one was there. It was there a second ago. I started walking back up the stairs and I heard the scream again, but it sounded like it was in the house. I turned around, the figure was there!

Ellie Allsup (14)
Stour Valley Community School, Clare

The Beginning Of Their End

Today was the last day before the summer holidays. The bell rang and I rushed out of school as fast as the wind. Smoke appeared. I couldn't see, then out of nowhere, I was standing in front of a raging volcano. I could hear a voice, a quiet voice, as quiet as a graveyard. I stealthily walked over. Right in front of me were my parents. I ran as fast as my legs could go. "You have one chance, choose wisely." I reached out for both of them, was this the beginning of their end?

Calum Steven Hayward (12)

Stour Valley Community School, Clare

I've Been Forgotten

I didn't believe it was me, I thought it was a great grandma or something. But then I looked at the date they'd died and it said January 2018 and no one had died in my family then. No one in my family had the same name as me.
I went home and, as I opened the door, everyone looked and my mum said, "It was probably just the wind." Then she shut the door and I was left outside in the freezing cold.
"I'm actually dead," I said to myself sadly.

Sarah Warbis-Rodda (11)
Stour Valley Community School, Clare

Last Place, Last Time

I waited for my friends, I waited for hours and they didn't turn up. I went inside and it was pitch-black, no lights were on. Suddenly, the lights flickered on and men shot at me. "Ouch!" I fell to the floor. I looked at my leg and I saw loads of batteries coming out. In my head, I thought that I had a fake leg. I ran home and told my mum all about it. My mum pulled my leg off and chucked it out the window. I screamed my head off while struggling towards my bedroom.

Jez Perry (13)
Stour Valley Community School, Clare

Memories

It had been six years since the president addressed the nation and had said those very words. Six years and yet, every day I hear that speech in my head. Six years and yet, every time I close my eyes, I see the fear and panic of that day. Sometimes vividly, with so much detail it feels more real than the present. I was tortured by dreams of the world. I used to know so much that, when I saw the dust-filled, forsaken wasteland that was the world, I wished I hadn't screamed...

George Clerkin (15)
Stour Valley Community School, Clare

They're Coming

I stepped back, knocking into a nearby gravestone. I ran into the church. I ran, pushing the creaky door open, and inside the darkly lit chamber. I slowly ran over to a window. There was something outside. Suddenly, I turned around and a hand grabbed my mouth. Everything went black as I fell.

When I woke up, I had a heart-wrenching pain in my leg. I looked up. Blood was everywhere. There was a man-eating zombie biting my leg off. I slowly closed my eyes in pain...

Harry Neads (13)

Stour Valley Community School, Clare

The Scream

It sounded like a scream of terror. I headed to my window and looked out. It was a misty night so I couldn't see much but there were two shadows at the bend on my street. One was holding a knife, the other was on the wall.
Suddenly, it went black and I heard one last scream and this time, it was one of pain. I sprinted back to my bed and covered myself. *What just happened?* I thought. *Could it happen to me?* At that moment, lightning struck...

Edward Chapman (11)
Stour Valley Community School, Clare

The Patient Grave

I stepped onto the grassy bank where the gravestone was and I stopped and stared at it. I could feel my insides bubbling up, I started to feel dizzy and sick. I was standing in front of the grave and, as I looked down, there was a hole with an open casket in it. I was drawn to it like a magnet. I could tell it was waiting for someone, there was no one else in the cemetery so there was no other answer except the obvious. I could tell it was waiting for me. This was it.

Katie Green (13)
Stour Valley Community School, Clare

Why?

Tears started to fill my eyes as I realised what I had done. I was told not to take the pill but my emotions got the better of me. Now I was stuck here forever in a world where I didn't exist, where I was dead!

The weather took a turn for the worst, it poured with rain. It soaked me to the skin, but I didn't care. I leaned over and looked at the gravestone, trying to remember what happened, but I could only remember taking the pill and nothing more...

Millie Wix (11)
Stour Valley Community School, Clare

You Have One Chance, Choose Wisely

I could see it every now and then as the mist began to clear, I knew I had to get it, but I needed a way of getting to the other side unseen. If I got caught, I knew my life would be over in a matter of seconds. I looked back and saw my little brother in tears. This happened every time he was able to see his rocking horse through the mist. I heard a scream coming from the other side of the mist. I needed to go while they were distracted. I made a run for it...

Sid Holmes (13)
Stour Valley Community School, Clare

That Scream That Echoed

Once I had a scream that echoed outside, it was a scream for help, for love. The school did not give me that help. I screamed inside and showed it outside, but still, no one helped. I screamed verbally as the pain got worse. Still, no one helped. They didn't help when I was having panic attacks longer than five minutes. I started having manic episodes and hearing voices that weren't there. That's when they started to help. It was too late...

Kale Anthony Aaron Woodley (15)
Stour Valley Community School, Clare

The Grave

I swept away the webs and dirt to see a date of when I died. It read, *1996-2010*. But now it's 2015. Therefore, I had already died. I went cold with fear. I heard banging, screaming, shouting, "Let me out! Help me!" I began to open the grave. It was empty. I looked around in confusion. My heart began to beat, getting louder and louder. Something touched my shoulder. I swiftly turned around, my heart stopped...

Darcy L'Estrange (15)
Stour Valley Community School, Clare

Dunno

The scream of a homeless but harmless man. I could tell he
was psyched up on drugs, drugs that messed with his mind.
He was prancing around like he was playing with fairies in
his own world. He staggered, fell and well, that was the end
of it.
Next thing I knew, the pigs were outside, making it look like
a crime scene. I knew I had to get out of here fast, before
the pigs came knocking.

Jayce Manning (15)
Stour Valley Community School, Clare

The Man

"You have one chance, choose wisely," he said to me. A red pill or a blue pill. He told me I could eat the red pill and my father would die, or the blue pill and my mother would die. "It's up to you, choose wisely," he said.

I replied, "My father." So I picked up the red pill and I put it in my mouth. Suddenly, the man flopped, dead.

Thomas Chaplin (14)
Stour Valley Community School, Clare

Our Finite Eternity

Isn't it an unsettling paradox that our hearts are trapped inside a box? Sticks and stones cannot break the cage's bones, yet flighty love can shatter in a matter of seconds the feather's firm promises. As you walked away from our finite eternity, I saw galaxies in your eyes. And me, little twinkle star, was lost in a sea of sunshine, guilty before pleading innocent at the bar. Some will say it is ironic that not only was it the last time my heart skipped a beat, but also my last one...

Alexia Collot d'Escury (15)
Swans International School, Calle Lago De Los Cisnes

The Night Of Hell

The night of hell, when the spirits, trolls, ghouls, and other whatnots come out of hiding. Everyone was rushing inside, doors slamming shut. The town clocktower shouted twelve times in the distance.

Midnight. Outsiders banged on doors, seeking shelter before the witching hour. The last window was locked and people behind doors silenced their children and hushed the candles, while a lonely, little girl stood on the unfamiliar road, tears rolling down her cheeks, for she didn't dare to wake the monsters.

Suddenly, a scream echoed outside. When the villagers glanced out of their windows, the streets were empty again...

Irina Burya (12)
The International School Of Moscow, Krylatskoe

Hallucinations

Crossing such a pristine desert was an entirely soulless endeavour, until we discovered something that defied belief. A white castle, growing like a crystal, sparkling just the same as any cut diamond, rose out of nothing to tower above us, disappearing into the freezing fog. Windowless perfection with a single entrance. The wind was silenced like a scolded dog. Then, not from the opening, but from the structure of the white castle came music in no form we had ever heard, in no language we could comprehend. Yet all at once, our legs walked again, taking us closer.

Darya Yushkevich (11)
The International School Of Moscow, Krylatskoe

Avatar

My avatar is logic. That's how I function. Black, or white. Up, or down. True, or false. Never both. That's how it works around here. But really, everything's grey. People are grey. Trust is grey.

Knowledge is grey. Everything I learned - a lie. I found out when I scratched myself, but instead of blood, there were wires. We're a simulation. But why don't I follow the rules? Because I'm a backend. And an eccentric. Grey. And the world is black. What happens when grey meets black? I'm about to find out. And I can't tell anyone.

Veronica Parakhin (13)
The International School Of Moscow, Krylatskoe

Last Breaths

'Get out now, while you still can', the skin-burning paper she had received said, concisely. It left her in absolute perplexity, as the scorching sun rays combed the glass windows of the restaurant, whose guests had no idea what the gods had in store for them.

She looked around for indication of jeopardy, however, none was to be seen. And then unexpectedly, out of the blue, there it happened. Her soul met with the victim of the tragic incident. All of the regrets she had inside herself, sunk deeper into her, as she drew in her last breaths.

Tereza Patockova (13)
The International School Of Moscow, Krylatskoe

Foundation

I fell. The windows of the skyscraper blended into a cartoon. I could see my reflection, even in the mirroring windows, I was falling to my death. Or was I? A moment before I hit the ground, I thought to myself, *what if the floor wasn't real? Bang!* I hit the ground as pain raced through my body, and yet, I was alive. In agony, I managed to stand up and look around. What I saw was beyond description, it was pitch-black, and yet I could see. Then it hit me, I'd reached the foundation, the beginning of the end.

Rodion Senko
The International School Of Moscow, Krylatskoe

Just Paper

It was barely sunrise when it happened. The wind ruffled my dishevelled hair as I sauntered across the jagged cobblestones. The sky was moonless, and ramshackle towers loomed over my vulnerable figure. *Rip!* A deafening sound engulfed me. I looked behind and watched as a long line tore all I had ever known. It was coming. I froze, urging myself to run. It wasn't long before I watched the sky tear. The shred reached me. My flesh was just paper, my blood was just ink. I could only hope that I would be written once more...

Mia Zeppenfeldt (13)
The International School Of Moscow, Krylatskoe

Purpose

They say I'm a traitor, but I prefer to call myself the creator of my destiny.

Food is scarce. I had no choice. The world is dying, that's a good excuse to start anew.

I sneaked into my brother's bunker. That was the first life I took. I took many more, leaving nothing behind me, save the rubble and lifeless bodies, some people very dear to me, some strangers. I may be a traitor, leaving my family in times of need, but everything has a purpose. That night, I found out mine was to kill and survive.

Sofia Kondratenko (12)
The International School Of Moscow, Krylatskoe

Double Identity

They say I am a liar, either I am not or I am a really good one. People assume constantly; they say they saw me somewhere I clearly don't recall going. Something gets stolen and the blame lands on me; someone disappears. *Creak!* A door to punishment opens. I walk into a room like a seeming criminal, the next day something is missing and still no memories. If I reach out for help, people ignore me or try but can't understand me. My only choice, get to the bottom of it. But who? How? Why?

Giulia Gardumi (13)
The International School Of Moscow, Krylatskoe

The Mist

The crackling of the fire and the smell of burning wood are transfixing me. In the distance, I can see a thick smear of mist. Something in my mind leads me towards the mist. I see hallucinations of a person in clothes which are tearing apart. I no longer control my body, the mist has hypnotised me. As my body is pulled into the mist, I see a hallucination of a hand engraving my name and seconds ticking down. Three, two, one. That's all I remember.

Maxim Yagnyatinskiy (13)
The International School Of Moscow, Krylatskoe

The End Is Here

He's gone, he's really gone. This means that the end is here. He was right, he was right all alone and now he's gone. It was always here, the end. There's no denying it. He's the one who saved me. He died saving me. His final words are still clear in my mind.

"Listen to me kid, be brave. You must save the world, because this is the beginning of the end. The world is gone, the apocalypse is here. The end is here."

Andrei Samarin
The International School Of Moscow, Krylatskoe

Some Stay, Some Go

It wasn't for me, but they wouldn't believe me. I had to protect them and that caused me to sacrifice a couple of friendships. Now, everything I do is an intentional movement, one wrong step and I'd be dead. But, had I stayed with the group, we'd have all died by now. If only I could've had the chance to explain myself to the others, those of which who have survived, that I have just saved them from the hell that Earth became.

Jayati Sood (14)
The International School Of Moscow, Krylatskoe

The War Cry

I remembered his last words, "This is the beginning of the end. The robots have taken over and we can't stop them. We have tried every single plan from A to Z and they have all failed, but we will not stop protecting what we love!" His delicate hand fell to his deathbed and we all bowed our heads.

"Oberon is right," I said. "This is not the end, it is only the beginning..."

Anastasia King (13)
The International School Of Moscow, Krylatskoe

Young**Writers**
Est.1991

YOUNG WRITERS INFORMATION

We hope you have enjoyed reading this book – and that you will continue to in the coming years.

If you're a young writer who enjoys reading and creative writing, or the parent of an enthusiastic poet or story writer, do visit our website **www.youngwriters.co.uk**. Here you will find free competitions, workshops and games, as well as recommended reads, a poetry glossary and our blog.

If you would like to order further copies of this book, or any of our other titles, then please give us a call or visit **www.youngwriters.co.uk**.

Young Writers
Remus House
Coltsfoot Drive
Peterborough
PE2 9BF
(01733) 890066
info@youngwriters.co.uk

 @YoungWritersUK    @YoungWritersCW